Malchus

Malchus

CHARLES WILLIAM JOHNS

RESOURCE *Publications* · Eugene, Oregon

MALCHUS

Resource Publications
An Imprint of Wipf and Stock Publishers
199 W. 8th Ave., Suite 3
Eugene, OR 97401

www.wipfandstock.com

PAPERBACK ISBN: 978-1-5326-1557-3
HARDCOVER ISBN: 978-1-5326-1559-7
EBOOK ISBN: 978-1-5326-1558-0

Manufactured in the U.S.A.   JANUARY 16, 2017 for my father Robert David Johns

I

I AM MALCHUS. I will put you in your place. At the expense of my actions you have yourselves a story, and if I am the protagonist I am also the antagonist. In fact I am mainly the jester, the fool, the drunken one. For your self-composed clear conscience, gentlemanly and naive, I have crucified myself. And far from literature being 'evil' it has become the law for me; it surveys me, keeps me in my place-the confession. So we both have our places, you and I, and far from wanting to be wrapped up in the story, I suggest you remain thoroughly out. Blood can spill from my hands to yours quite easily from a turn of the page (or from closing this book in disgust). The written word has a habit of unsticking itself from its page and gallivanting about as if it were your very own conscience.

Why is it that we return, again and again, to books, as if there were some insight to be gained, as if we could bypass experience, the *consequence* of experience, the consequence of actions and decisions in this very real world we attempt to shield ourselves from? It is as if we were naive enough to think that knowledge could be gained without a loss. Every emotion is a disturbance of some kind. The intricacies of loss is an art form and I am happy to have suffered so that you may enjoy the 'pleasure of the text'.

Every sensation, every mode of enjoyment, is a mode of communication; one says "I like this", or, "why did you sting me nettle?" But to *who* are we communicating with in these frivolous human scenarios? Perhaps to each other? Our inner-selves? God? And so the history of life becomes the history of a conversation, spanning miles and miles, echoing even further into caverns, cata-combs, connecting burning stars to our stratosphere through the instrument of human perception, uniting insects rattling in bushes between the footsteps of a young man's morning walk. In this sense everyone knows everyone, we have all spoken to each other in this life, we have all expressed something to everyone, and-for now-I become known; my little voice is heard over a blizzard of premature utterances. Very well. The entirety of human existence is one voice fighting over another.

II

I WALK ACROSS THE West Common, towards my father's house. I had drunk just enough to transform the pervasive sirens of police cars into an indifferent whir. I label the sirens 'city sounds' and in doing so I can successfully compartmentalise the fear that such sirens bring. Once successfully compartmentalized I can proceed to shut down that particular part of the brain. I had drunk one less than my limit (I wanted to drink that last one, to resolve it) and so I could continue acting amicably; so I could act like myself *before* the incident.

There is nothing more guilt-invoking than a beautiful summers day. It is as if-in appearing that one day too late-it were teaching you a lesson; "look at what you could have basked and folicked in, if only you were a free man". Instead the sun sticks to my skin and clothes, makes everything all too apparent. The sun is always the first to spot a criminal, it shines on me the most. It's irritating obnoxious rays of transparent clarity also reflects itself inside the human being, in the bad conscience. That bad place inside of all of us (and most hidden from ourselves) transforms into a prism, cleansed out by the kaleidoscopic beatitude of natural light. This light, affirming itself as the 'clear light of day', that light which makes us hate what we have done in the night. This light, working itself into my pores, trying to clean me out!

One can get carried away in the night, it is almost advisable that one go down with the sun into an evening of confusion, where one cannot distinguish between feelings and forms, where one does not know who one is, who fools themselves into thinking that he is part of the night itself, an expression of it. When there is no clear light of day anything could happen, and you can blame it on the stars or the chugging of a freight train. Where one is standing there, half-drunk, wondering whether their desire can outreach their territory, whether it can soar above the small town that conditions them, whether it can reach beyond the train tracks, and you say to yourself "did a part of me leave with that passing train"? One may truly burn at night like a firefly but one must hide like an antique rug in an unused dusty spare room when the sun comes out, when the sun comes up to judge its denizens, spotting the dust particles that now appear dancing in mid-air from the archaic movement of trouble that came with the eventide. The sun ascends to witness a broken world, and the morning appears as if a group of guilty children saying that "it was not us".

I walk as quickly as I can to my father's house wishing I were a dog that could take the many subterranean, un-colonized trails that have escaped human sight. Several metres before I reach the front door and I hear a siren that pierces into my nervous system. I halt. The siren starts and stops as if it were intentionally trying to get my attention. Is this the siren that gets me? How do you know which siren is yours? Is it a siren that only you can hear? Is it that siren which is in sync with the beating of one's heart? Are they the same thing? The moral alarm of the subjective heart mirrored by an automaton that thinks it is carrying out the word of God, the word of the State. The archaic heart deep within weeds and ancient ivory, tormented by the tower blocks of police sensibility.

I react, all at once. I am scarred. The fear, not on the surface of the heart but underneath somehow-the hearts underbelly. And the stomach, suddenly impregnated with fear as if it were a giant heart itself-a whale's heart in pain-mourning. This is my siren. How do I know? It is oriented towards me, it knows my location, it is trying to catch me much like the sirens of the sea. And what does this encounter actually designate? When the internalised fear of being caught is apprehended by exteriority. What is this exact point where paranoia is affirmed by fate? It is so hard not to comply with fate, it is rather like trying to stop yourself from crying-"let it out, be caught, the worst is over". Am I somehow safe then? No, I go to jail!

The police car drives past me. It was perhaps even an ambulance. I cannot know anything in this perpetual state of anxiety. I would rather let innocent victims die from severe wounds out on the pavement than see police cars and ambulances parade themselves around the streets I walk upon quietly.

I go round the back of the house. Underneath the plant pot on the table, just as my father had said, was the backdoor key. I let myself in and immediately grab the garage key which has been placed thoughtfully upon the kitchen windowsill. I muttered the words I told myself the following night; that it had been "at least forty eight hours since the incident, and if someone wanted to arrest me then they would have done it by now . . . and it would be good-possibly even healthy-for you to accept working for your father this morning-which entails listening to old classical music on vinyl in order to discern whether any of them are scratched (and hence thrown in the 'discard' pile), or, clearly audible (perhaps excellent, excellent +, even possibly near-mint) and hence fit for re-sale". I would listen to these records in a shed far far away from the crime scene, in a respectable estate, as if I were a completely different person unaffiliated with the crime. Perhaps I had knocked my head, been diagnosed with amnesia. Perhaps I could simply act like I had amnesia, for the rest of my life, or , perhaps, if I try hard enough, I could lose myself in classical music, be drawn into the circle of its repetitions, and forget who I am.

I picked up the first record from the pile of records left out for me and put it on the turnstyle. Sibelius quartets. After the steady, slow confirmation of needle and shellac a perfect quartet gradually formed. At first one viola cutting through a space set up for melody, acutely and angularly it created one wall of sound. A violin giddily sprung from underneath this first wall, in a gap between the floorboards, or on the floor I myself was sitting on. It began to say something but then it wasn't sure, and began to partly form another wall. Then a cello resounded as if it were already in the room/song but waiting its turn. It became the soil and then the floorboards, and finally a third wall. I looked out upon my father's garden from inside the garage, through the garage door I had left open. Finally a single violin soared within these three walls-"the shrill of this violin was me" I thought to myself. As quickly as it had affirmed its place within the room it suddenly transformed into a police siren, one closer than ever before. The quartet had lured me into the security of song (like how a scared child sings to itself in the woods to keep itself company). I got up and headed towards what felt like a giant hole filled with sunlight and nature. I stood there, on the threshold of the garage door, painfully (I had no shoes on and the threshold dug into the soles of my feet). I stood completely upright and spread my arms out as if I were composing Sibelius' quartet. Siren upon siren proliferated, each glimmer of the sun cascading and reflecting off all objects from the ground up, showing that they were part of everything, welcoming everything. And the police? What did it matter now? Every part of nature expressed an immanent force equal to the power of the police-expressing a similar law. Everything was perpetual incandescence, I could not see where one started or began. Rising and falling, con-tracting and retracting, accumulating and dispersing through one unitary rhythm. Every reflective surface, whether window, tarmac, vase, drop of dew, collided together and resembled the rear-view mirrors of police cars. And within such windows-reflections of reflections-lay cool policemen and policewoman made up of com-plete prosthesis; simulated in uniform, mediated by walki-talkies, covered in hats and chiselled features like terrifying cartoons, and in one breath-like any great composer-I changed the universe.

Standing still upon this threshold, with bruised soles, I took a deep breath, and much of the world came in with me;

A woman in high heels walking down a boulevard, a butcher cutting meat, a skateboard leaning against a concrete pillar, a cat falling asleep, a couple walking into a cinema, an old man undress-ing, a clown in repose, a teacher walking towards his car after a long day at work, the sound of a family of sparrows in-between the footsteps of an angry teenager crying, a stainless steel water fountain, a child kicking a football, a man upon a step ladder . . .

When I finally exhaled I had forgotten how long I had been standing there, whether it was the true exhalation to the first inhalation, or whether I had been breathing steadily for some time. Everything had changed, only Sibelius had stayed the same. The women's high heels cracked and broke apart, she fell, and the beads on her handbag scattered everywhere conceivable, forever irretrievable. The butcher had cut his thumb off and a fountain of plum coloured blood sprung out and covered bits of meat. The skateboard suddenly began to lose grip of the column, dropped and caressed the pillar before rolling away. The cat yawned and started licking itself. The cinema-goers stopped still before the automatic doors, which appeared broken. The old man heard a scream from across the road. The clown thought about his mother and why he called her Diana and not mother. The teacher got a sudden erection. The family of sparrows transported to another neighborhood as if they had entered some crack in the fabric of space-time. The teenager crying saw a girl in yellow laughing. The water fountain was vandalized abruptly but articulately. A kid in phoenix scored his first goal. The stepladder fell.

Everything balanced on a moment, as if time were a series of edges that one fell from. It stopped being a problem which side you fell, as long as it were downward.

I was mid-way through eating an apple when I had first thought there to be a police car outside. I stood on 'that' threshold for a few moments and then returned to the record player to put on Benjamin Britten's Nocturne. When I continued to chew the apple it tasted differently from the one I was eating before.

III

I LEAVE AT AROUND five o'clock, before my father returns home from work. I walk back the same way, across the common. It is evening now, the sun has set. I walk as if I were slushing through the paint of *Wheatfield with Crows*. I cannot return to the garage (that is-*my* garage). 'It' is in there. Red chalk and dust is still in the air from when it happened. And only *one* lock has been fastened. It would only take a homeless man or a drunk to stumble by, see that it is only half locked, prize it open . . . I couldn't even bare the thought of seeing his reaction-Christ Almighty! It is really only a small lock, no better than a cheap bike lock. And drunk men always sleep in the lots opposite mine. Well where should I go?! What should I do?! I cannot even go to the university, the fashion department. I spent too many nights up in that room, brooding, and it's all on camera! If men cannot master their own thoughts then these cameras will! I tell you, it is ironic and absurd. Yesterday I was walking down Steep Hill and I became aware of the many cameras attached to the corners of buildings that were surveying me. My free and easy movements were re-oriented by the realization of these looming eyes. I was darting from one side of the road to the other, pathetically pirouetting down the hill. These cameras, from wanting to survey my every move, in-fact determined them! "How has this game helped anyone?" I shout to one of the cameras, looking upward as if I were talking to a Diplodocus. It was only then, with this visceral address, that the camera face turned away. Did I beat it, did I stare it down, or, did it reject me? They do not know my sin. They do not even know what blood is. They just turn their heads about like children or dogs in perennial distraction. However, in the end there is no innate difference between things. In death we are all revealed as the same-nothing.

I dare not even *speak* to anyone, for danger that I might suddenly spill the whole truth out. But what a wonderful truth it is! A truth that could heal others. But one must hide miracles for fear of being burnt at the stake, crucified. Men have invested too much of their time moulding the world into edible chunks for me to go and ruin such banality with *the impossible*! For it is true that, the more deeply a man expresses himself and his predicament, the more unreadable he becomes, the more misunderstood he is, the more bizarre he seems, the more reason he should be 'dealt with'. Truth has a funny way of attaching itself to a person (for fear of being abused and mocked by the masses) and I will stay faithful to its secret. Yes, truths have secrets just like lies. Do not forget that there is always a universe of consequences surrounding the event of a truth. A truth hard to swallow, a truth that cannot be monopolized upon. What an unthinkable amount of consequences for this little beauty of a truth I have stumbled upon.

Like Job before me, I know that in my torment there is a sovereign virtue. I simply must not blurt it out like a child who thinks he is a comedian. So I cannot go anywhere. I cannot go home (to my garage . . . where 'it' lies), nor the university (where there is ample tables and chairs for studying, free water and electric heating) because they have their eyes on me. I am stranded because of this truth. All of a sudden I felt drowsy and irritable. It was still hot out even though the sun had settled amongst the trees bordering the golf course in the distance. I decided to continue what I was doing before I arrived at my fathers, and so entered the nearest pub.

I could not think of ever being redeemed for my actions. I could not see where one goes after such a crime either. There was some solace in accepting this however. I may have to sink into a new life, push myself to the bottom like an anchor, settle here in this strange world beyond good and evil, beyond aspiration and ego, beyond the living. But this is the place where most of us dwell on a day to day basis.

I looked at the bar lady and tapped one of the beer bumps with my forefinger. I took too long to collect the precise change and instead decided to give her what I had, covered in sweat, turning my wallet inside out, looking for more coins. I heard a final coin drop from out of my wallet onto the bar. It was a small key that unlocked one of the padlocks to the garage. I felt immediately cautious. I was ready to kill her if she were to so much as glance at it for more than a few seconds. I placed it quickly back in my wallet and noticed she had left a pile of change on the bar for me. She was already serving another customer and there was my pint.

I sat on one of the tables outside and soon felt my sanctity abused by two women, who had just stepped out into the beer garden, raping the world with their laughter, running their fingers through their hair, playing with themselves, turning the universe into something deceitful, pernicious. I was extremely attracted to them. After sitting for a while I got out my notebook and started writing . . .

IV

A Girl/Woman.

When did laughter stop denoting the uttermost depths of horror, joy, intoxication? When did laughter stop being a practice of overcoming the ghosts of the world and the ghosts of oneself? And when did it become a method of territorialization? When did laughter become a form of commodity? A girl's/woman's laughter promotes the quality of the bourgeois. A girl's/woman's laughter automatically advertises all the laughter industries that have conditioned her social role-her nonchalance. To laugh is to be accepted/acceptable. One is understood in humour. In many situations it is the epitome of comprehension, the condition for contact between individuals. Humour is mainly feminine now. The girl/woman laughs and thereby produces a consensus; a consensus where parameters are drawn-inside is humour and outside is non-humour. Her usually light, fluttery laughter never expresses joy but only represents it. It must fall within that arbitrary neutral middle between a sigh and a cackle. It must be calm and controlled like an artwork. It must give off an allusion to spontaneity, like the flapping of a startled butterflies wings, but be as considered as a puff of perfume. Laughter is perfume.

One is taught what to laugh at and how to laugh at it, the style changing subtly like the style of fashion. Humour has dominated every aspect of communality today. When one does not react or answer by laughing then one is almost anticipating laughter from the other party. We talk in restaurants, gardens, and in our beds as if we were talking in an elevator. One in-fact needs humour desperately in order to convey a sense of continuity-the designation of a law. Humour is a wall that man clings to in the dark. I will attempt to go on but I find it so despicable.

One covers up an embarrassment by laughter. One laughs at themselves in fear of being a victim *of* laughter. But they should attain a level of purity, of vulnerability, which affords them the capacity to laugh at oneself. It is actually a vicious circle; the condition for embarrassment is a humour whose purpose it is to humiliate. One should ask why something is 'embarrassing' in the first place, and they will always find some presupposition, some social rearing point its ugly head like a stupid monolith. There is a resentment in laughter; it is used to designate a weakness, an unorthodoxy, but the unorthodoxy is never found, only gaps in the orthodoxy, only boundaries where humour and sense stop (.. but that is the place of hilarity)!

Humour is an attempt to make failure insignificant. Because failure and futility is all around us we anxiously designate all chaos as humorous. To laugh at oneself is to pretend that you were in-fact *not* the victim of humiliation; you betray yourself and become an alter-ego through laughter, mocking yourself, mocking the weak. The compulsion to laugh at oneself is essentially the refutation/ prostitution of oneself for the production of laughter; one gains a consensus through mutual laughter whilst negating their very being. You are the laughter of yourself but not yourself (the Christian self is shocked by your prostitution, stares vacantly, impotently-the silence between laughter). Humour has also become an etiquette that one cannot afford to go without. It is a process of determination. We are slaves to it. Humours criteria is mass conformism and its orientation is steered by 'the powers that be'-HBO, Fox, people high enough to laugh down at us.

The anachronism is the product of a much more subtle, conniving process; the past must become laughable because it is not in synchronicity with our present. One must make what one does not understand humorous.

A strong humour comes from deep inside the subject (a vacillating 'thing' accumulating power within oneself). Caligula on the beach-*what* he is laughing at we will never know, it is invisible, the epitome of the impossible. We cannot deduce, from the beach or Caligula, any reason for laughter. There is no simple cause here. Laughter is an addition and cannot be reduced to an object (the object of titillation). Laughter used to be the surplus of a situation, an excess, so powerful it could change the very rules navigating subject and object. Does Edvard Munch's *Scream* not perpetually echo out like the repetitious dialect of laughter? And does this not change, transform, produce the landscape? Does it not turn everything inside out?! Like the constant folding of oxygen back into itself, the acceleration of breathing in and out finds a point where one does not know which is which, it cannot be located on either side.

The other type of humour is a weak, sick, contagious one. It almost has a mathematical accuracy and consistency to it. It does not come from inside, it comes from televisions, fashion, clothes, coffee cups, 'friends'. It sprawls itself out neutrally like modern paving stones. It is extremely relative; weak humour is constructed piecemeal-a sentence, a question, a reference. It constructs itself like a virtual modelling programme; each line connects to the next, plots an etiquette of humour, designates boundaries. Weak humour wants to expand, it wants to *be us*. It wants to be the prostheses of the modern human world; it wants to carry on without us. Already we are seeing men and woman being entirely absorbed, manipulated, designated by humour; a woman's relationship to the social world becomes a 'giving-in', a compliance, to the synaptic links that humour creates. On situations, men, objects-it is purposive by its own accord. One day aliens will discern this weak humour as 'a theory of distraction'. This rule of laughter is neither Pagan nor, obviously, Christian. The laughter of the world is completely meaningless. If it were meaningful we would not be laughing.

I have witnessed only one great triumph of this weak humour, to the extent where I have to ask whether it was not perhaps the strong kind hiding in contemporaneity. Oh how it transformed, from yet another remark in the swamp of arbitrary institutional humour, to take flight like a kite, a striped kite. It was so much more rewarding than that tolerable form of humour clever people have inherited called cynicism. Anyway, this strong humour I witnessed, with striped colours, you might even say it were a firework, yet it was throwaway, but not in the modern banal sense but rather in the *mystical* sense; its humour said to me; "I have too much of it, an excess, so I give it away . . . and that's that". The place and gesture where this humour sprung forth from (or accidentally escaped into) was utopia. It all lasted but a few moments. I was sitting on a bench (as I do) and saw a middle aged couple walking towards me. Behind them was a girl on a bike with stabilizers. I hardly even noticed the couple (perhaps with a pram?). Anyway, a few bird tweets and roaming car sounds later and there came this girl on her bicycle. I was looking my usual serious self, verging on sadness, and she looked up at me, read my facial expression and somehow-with a perfect mixture of parody and endearment-mimicked my facial expression. To see this blue-eyed, freckle-faced beautiful girl take on my persona, my burden, my humility, my seriousness (!), bore a truth so incongruous to me I felt it as a revelation. "Yes I am a silly serious man am I not young one"? Oh how she singlehandedly mocked and defeated all my gloomy gods in that one parodic, angelic expression. All of them; Montaigne, Dostoevsky, Freud, Benjamin, Adorno, Levinas, Camus, Bataille, Baudrillard . . . what could they do now?! And then, in seeing me 'crack' and let out a smile (so natural it felt like water running down a stream) she immediately burst into the most beautiful smile I had ever seen. Not just aesthetically beautiful but a smile that acted as if it were a sky full of oxygen to a squadron of drowning men. A smile that felt undoubtedly connected to some truly good deed being done. And she knew, in her parodic smile, that she would make me smile beforehand! Oh goddess of joy, laughter and forgetting! I have tried to sit and think through this cunning effect of impossible joy but a wall always appears; beyond the wall is perhaps love without rationality nor selfishness-Christian love?

A love without thought perhaps, but antithetical to lust. And how did she know she would succeed?! Perhaps if I were to remain with a morbid expression she would have simply copied that and then carried on peddling? That would have also been magnificent! But not as much so! She could not have lost to my sadness even if she tried. There is something beautiful in confidence after all! She was the harbinger of new 'moods', new childish things, a 're-evaluation of all values'. And in reflection I wished to have said this to her; "I know I am just another of your apostles and you do not need me, but I wanted to tell you that you will be fine, because I love you, and this is from someone who loves no-one, no-one but you, my daughter of Jairus, my Dounia. And if you were to smile at me like you did before, I think I might die. Too much light for a man who writes notes from the underground. But bless you . . . and leave swiftly. I want your presence to be as short and precise as life itself. Please go, before I realize that my heart has extended and transformed into my whole body, my brain, those trees over there, before I lose myself in the truth; that love has no proximity."

V

I STOP WRITING AND close the notepad slowly and securely as if something had been resolved. I tap its cover signalling a gesture of appreciation for that last experience. Perhaps I tap the cover of the notepad as if I were patting a deceased relative in a coffin at a funeral, their cold knuckles being the notepads ring bound spine. I look up. The women had left, leaving behind American colours and drinks. It is much greyer now. The comfort of Britain returned to me and all one can do is hardly acknowledge it. I finish my pint of beer and head out confidently, as if I know where I am going. I do not know where I am going.

I walk across the golf course and down the Brayford towards town. I think about life and death as if they were different settings on Christmas tree lights. The world is so relentless that death could never be seen as a stopping or slowing down of it. Life has no time for death. In the event of death the phenomenon of it gets picked up, moved along, like a dog picking up a stick with its jaws. Death is ridiculed by life; turned into artefacts, funerary rites, turned into words and memories that humans find mournful. In other words, death is given a type of life. The closest thing we can experience to death are things we do not know about such as black holes and the bottom of the deepest darkest oceans. Instead we make death a type of uniquely human loss which embodies the world and its culture, similar to any living thing. In a sense nothing ever died, that is, no one ever experienced this thing called 'death'. At that point where a dying man is grasping onto those last moments of life, at that point where he closes his eyes and waits to experience it, he instead dies without experiencing it. The experience is terminated before being experienced, because you have to be alive to experience things.

The only thing real is the crime, the act of murder. That can be *experienced*, made informative, celebrated. It changes the life of the murderer more than the life of the murdered. In this banal, neutral world there are only things that are guilty or not guilty. There is no rest for those that are guilty . . . wicked. Everything is animated by this section of society, this special gene. They are the only ones capable of equalling life. I promise you there is nothing more to this flat piece of paper entitled existence. We have refused this fact for so long, made the paper into brightly set colours, turned this paper into commodities, extensions of our own resentment and desire like infinitely extended origami objects. And then we just move them around, inch by inch, hoping that they will transform our world, into something beautiful.

A police car had parked in the middle of the street roughly five metres ahead of me. I was immediately sick in the Fossdyke Canal. I spat the last bits of sick out into the water and watched them float off like stupid children at a water-ride in Florida. I looked up and smiled at the policeman. Such an offensive vehicle *they* drive about in; offensive to aesthetics I mean. Too many colours for one object. What is it? Blue, red, yellow, white . . . is there orange in there somewhere? How sickly I thought. Is it contagious? It is far removed from the colours of the Roman law. Things had to die in order for us to create colour. The red dye used to produce deep crimson, coming from the guts of the Armenian cochineal, colours stemming from their geological milieux, plants, insects, colours of the Mediterranean.

The colours of today are far removed from everything. It would be punishment enough to be chauffeured about in such a thing. I laughed, perhaps disturbingly. The policeman turned around and looked in my direction. I glanced down at the floor and then followed the floating sick downstream with my eyes.

Later I began to see these constabulary colours everywhere; in every manufactured product a colour appeared. First as a printed surface, and then perhaps as a simulation of colour, these simulations pointing to ghosts of prior sensations. Where these colours come from I do not know. Was there once a world where colour existed as truth and not merely the representation of an image? Some other world perhaps, expressed through vivid pigments, crammed full with sensation? But such a world didn't *appear* to be reigning within the world we had made. Infact this world of pure colour seemed imprisoned by a strange human instrumentality; making colour an upgrade, an embellishment, bridled to the objects we desire, making such desirable.

I wondered to myself if the world would miss the parts that I had taken from it. If I should replace the things that I had stolen from it and used. Do people not recognize the gaps in the world of the 'everyday' that I have left?

I walk over the university bridge and spot the fashion department on the second floor of the Art & Design building. It stands at the end of the corridor and from the outside you can see it jut out like the cockpit of a spaceship, as if the entire building were infinitely deliberating flight. Does it know that one of its rooms has one less object in it? Do the students? I thought this unlikely because it was the summer holidays and most students had returned to their families. Do the gardens of The Lawn know that I have pulled something out of it, from its soil? What a humiliating patch of soil I must have left there. What blessed natural colours have I deflowered for myself, for Tracey.

It is not enough to 'loose him and let him go' (John 11:44, Fourth Gospel), one must be mended and dressed. "Replacing old objects", I said to myself, "I will be giving everyone a *new* object! Finally, a new object that corresponds to the concept, the abstract, the universal, the ideal! And no one will be looking around foolishly and selfishly for misplaced objects such as stationary and money, no, instead they will be fixed in their comprehension". I utter calmly that "it is my secret and my faith". And I am to stare into her, because of the things that I have done, because of my *nihilism* (or rather because

I still care deeply about meaning, in a world where it has been trivialized). This is my burden, this is my 'millstone hung around my neck' (Matthew 18:6, First Gospel). Christ comes to all his herd that listen, prayers are always received personally, but a nihilist *struggles* with God through raw experience.

VI

I DECIDED TO WALK uphill towards the Bailgate. Perhaps the art gallery is still open. I ask myself again-"to whom does the police siren call to? To whose presence does it command"? It is antithetical to the presence of a royal court ballet, their presence is to the king, queen and their noblemen. Their presence is also the presence of being in the moment (the present), that is to say, the affirmation of music and dance. The only present that these policemen have achieved is a captured present that is nullified through fear and banal procedure. There is no reflexivity in this technique, no sensibility. They are incongruous with their surroundings unlike music and dance and therefore achieve no harmony. Because they are all these things they can never be artistic. Perhaps all lower classes of men are personified by the police. You know, those men that are conservative in their ideas, conservative in their routine of 'what-it-is-that-they-have-been-allocated-for', with an extremely base personality, who do not know the art of deception or the power of their own ego. Men that are the handmaidens of society and not vice versa. Men ruled by external objects and surroundings, men that do not follow ideas through, nor their thinking. A completely different phenomenon of 'non-thinking' occurs within these men, as if it were the byproduct of some deeper more determinate process untouched from intention and creativity. Men that see X and think X in whatever way X has been conditioned to be seen as. Their thinking is merely the conjunctive synthesis of an object. They have 'frog perspectives'. This synthesis never reaches thought.

The predicament of being human is a thoroughly abstract one, that is, it is a predicament that arises regardless of objects; it does not need objects for such a predicament. It goes without saying-then-that any transformation in society will never vanquish the absolute suffering, the diagnosis, of the human condition. Anyway, these base men are the bedrock of civilization; they are one long scurrying crust of the earth, inert in their senseless clamour, signalling death in every lethargic domestic activity, yet never equalling it. They are *policemen*. Have you not noticed that this metaphor is attempting to be literally realised by the government? 'Proletariats' that work for the Council, who throughout the early hours of the day emerge as policemen in yellow uniform, fixing some fractured, stammering object such as the buttons that operate pedestrian crossings, a street lamp etc. Or those green cousins of the yellows that place fines across the windshields of resting idle cars. There is also that specimen who clear the falling leaves of our last beautiful autumn, cleaning things that do not desire to be cleaned. The whole world is in uniform.

It is almost as if this world of uniform men, in their ignorance, are building a house of cards for us independent nobleman to knock down. Again and again this has happened in history. Perhaps it is the most natural way ('dialectics' as Hegel called it). Socrates, Caesar, Christ, Napoleon, Nietzsche have all changed the game, have been elitists, in both their inevitable dispute with the common consensus, but also in their desire to attain public distribution of their ideas.

I find it humorous how we have our waves of little Marxists, indoctrinated by infallible structural theories and systems, their liberalisms and democracies, their boring utopias, and then suddenly a benefactor comes along and plots his palace grounds, his mini-capitalisms.

The truth, that many writers, poets and philosophers attempt to hide, is that us 'free spirits' actually prefer the buildings and streets of the elite, the fascist. We wonder about their beautiful monoliths like nihilist flaneurs. We love to look up high towards the roofs of buildings. We love to get lost in a world made by someone else.

And us *criminals* do not simply disobey the laws of social conduct, but also, more dangerously, the laws of certain *concepts* under which such behaviours function, become legitimate; utilitarianism-dictums that abolish the individual and the qualitative for the quantitative, dictums that pathetically exclaim "we are in this together", the impetus of mass conformism which results in a totalising desire for the accumulation of luxuries, commodities. My only solace is that all these people will die at some point without ever really living, and they won't get another chance, and I will be there pointing and laughing, shouting "Ha Ha"! And I will deserve this 'last laugh' because I have been in a lake naked at midnight, because I have tried to escape who I am to the extent that blisters have covered the entirety of my feet and have stopped me from walking further, because I have fallen in love and have given myself over to terrible thoughts, because I know simultaneously how worthless and profound I am, because sometimes I hear God and then at other times I hear the emptiness of him as if someone had said something awkward at a dinner party.

Regardless of all these refined observations I am still *guilty*. Christians are prescribed to feel guilty-this is what gives them weight and purpose (a life of attempted repent). They have an extremely clear insight into the sin of the western world. They realise that they too are responsible for that misery, that they too have to be blamed, if only through compliance (of being born). And whom did they replace in their being born? This is another guilt that plagues the mind of the true Christian.

Us Christians have a sense of justice which is at odds with despotic laws. Our law is inside, theirs is outside. There is no real justice for the proper Christian, just overwhelming love and knowledge of the line that demarcates faith from non-faith (incredulity). This is their compass. We hope that one will find their way, and by himself. The police is antithetical to this attitude. They first of all pretend to be God by exerting power (the worst of God is when he exerts power). We deal in sin which is absolute, and they deal in civil disobedience which is relative to whatever despotic system is functioning at that particular time. When it comes to 'disobedience' we are perhaps even Pagan; we say "oh let them frolic and learn, so he stole a loaf of bread to feed his family . . . he has good conscience, he is simply learning his way in and around society". And what if we take this Paganism to its extreme, to murder? We would say that "the man who is no longer with us is better off than the man who lives with the burden of this guilt . . . he will be forced to die twice . . . no thrice. His conscience dies in the act of murder, and after taking a man's life he will have to hold onto his spectre as well, and then finally he has his own death to worry about". Trust me when I say this.

But we have ourselves a conflict of epic proportions weighing down on us. The conflict is between what has been called *The Two Great Commandments* found in Matthew, Gospel One, 22:36–40:

> *Jesus said unto him, Thou shalt love the Lord thy God with all thy heart, and with all thy soul, and with all thy mind. This is the first and* great commandment. *And the second is like unto it, Thou shalt love thy neighbour as thyself. On these* two commandments *hang all the law and the prophets.*

With these two commandments hang all the drama of the Prophets, Apostles and Christians. What it generates is a question, a decision; what if my love for my neighbour exceeds that of God himself? What if there became a situation where I had to decide, protect one from the other?

Eliphaz the Temanite secretly loved Job more than God (the term 'loyal love' can be traced back to *The Arrival of the Three Comforters* in the Book of Job (2:11–13)) and Job's suffering made Eliphaz worship Man in ways that he could not have comprehended before encountering him covered in boils head to toe.

> *Now when Job's three friends heard of all this adversity that come upon him, they came each one from his own place. Eliphaz the Temanite, Bildad the Shuhite and Zophar the Naamathite; and they made an appointment together to come to sympathize with him and comfort him. When they lifted up their eyes at a distance and did not recognize him, they raised their voices and wept. And each of them tore his robe and they threw dust over their heads toward the sky. . . .*

And so it begins-a secret trajectory of mortal man, relentlessly perishable men, believing in one another, believing in their greatness, forging bonds underneath stellar skies:

> Star friendship.-*We were friends and have become estranged. But that was right, and we do not want to hide and obscure it from ourselves as if we had to be ashamed of it. We are two ships, each of which has its own goal and course; we may cross and have a feast together, as we did-and then the good ships lay so quietly in one harbour and in one sun that it may have seemed as if they had already completed their course and had the same goal. But then the almighty force of our projects drove us apart once again, into different seas and sunny zones, and maybe we will never meet again-or maybe we will, but will not recognize each other: the different seas and suns have changed us! That we had to become estranged is the law above us; through it we should come to have more respect for each other-and the thought of our former friendship should become more sacred! There is probably a tremendous invisible curve and stellar orbit in which our different ways and goals may be included as small stretches-let us rise to this thought! But our life is too short and our vision too meagre for us to be more than friends in the sense of that sublime possibility.-Let us then believe in our star friendship even if we must be earth enemies.*[1]

The impetus to take this decision seriously can be found within every great story. What we have is a man who rebels against the State, the Law, God, rebels against the common consensus, even genetic heritage and family, in order to help his 'brother', his 'neighbour'. The traces of this decision can be found in Antigone when she is banished from the kingdom and locked in a tomb, eventually hanging herself, because she disobeyed the law that states no mourning or proper burial of her brother Polynices. It is found in Anne Frank's helpers (her Apostles). It is found in the circumstance of two true lovers (Romeo and Juliet, Antony and Cleopatra). Are not the Apostles themselves a group of brothers, a

---

1. Friedrich Nietzsche, Aphorism 279, *The Gay Science*, 1882.

collection of unique personalities rebelling against the status quo? Yes, Christianity is contra the police. Let us not forget the conspiracy against Jesus by the Jewish chief priests and the 'teachers of the law' (i.e the police).

> *Now the Passover and the Festival of Unleavened Bread were only two days away, and the chief priests and the teachers of the law were scheming to arrest Jesus secretly and kill him.*[2]

We also know-and sometimes try to forget-that Christianity is also contra Capitalism :

> *Jesus entered the temple courts and drove out all who were buying and selling there. He overturned the tables of the money changers and the benches of those selling doves.*[3]

I want to exclaim "God does not exist", or, "he hath no purchase on me". I wish to rejoice in saying "I am trying to find my friend, those sensitive ones, and simply their presence will rid me of all my deep unfathomable anxieties".

---

2. Mark, Gospel Two, 14:1

3. Matthew, Gospel Two , 21:12

VII

Before I had a chance to take in the scenery of the historic Bailgate area, I realised I had already walked through it and had now reached the art gallery. I faced the automatic doors and to my surprise they had opened. It was far past closing time, and I had only flirted with the idea of visiting the galleries facade, as a passing attraction before heading to the nearest pub or bar. But there it was, opening, as if just for me, and I could hear sophisticated laughter coming from the courtyard gallery wing. I entered. I was feeling lethargically rebellious. I knew some of the staff there, and when it suited me (moments like this) I could slip in as part of the crowd.

I was confronted immediately by a small fat lady who, it seemed, had mastered her front of house monologue.

"Hello sir, Have you come for the private exhibition"?

I just said "yes".

"Delighted to have you. On behalf of the Indoctus Foundation, in partnership with The Collection, we have a very special selection of work for you by young emerging British talent who have been nominated for the East Midlands Innovation Award. Please follow the hall round to your left and help yourself to a complimentary glass of champagne".

I simply responded-after a short pause-with another "yes" and proceeded towards the exhibition space.

Luckily the table displaying glasses of wine was not inside the courtyard gallery wing but, rather, stood in the hall parallel to the exhibition space. I quietly walked over to the solitary table (supporting two meagre glasses of champagne) and picked up one of them. Looking through the doorframe, into the gallery space, I could just about see the vibrating shoulders of people, covered in cotton, silk, tweed, leather, and sometimes nothing. I was content with this and carried on drinking. It was already obvious, from the affable clamour, that it was indeed the guests who paraded themselves around as the artworks; seducing each other with the sounds of their jangling bracelets, the flinging of silk scarves, the repositioning of spectacles, subtle forms of capture through various witticisms. The actual artworks seemed to hang quietly, almost ghostlike in the background, and if they had been blessed with mouths they would have hung half open, ajar, like children filled with misunderstanding. Suddenly a face popped into the right hand side of the exhibition entrance as if she were a puppet in a pantomime perfectly framed by the open door. She began, like they all do, with strange sounds and gestures, as if something were imminent. Something is always imminent to these people.

"Well do come in. We need an outsider's perspective on this work exhibited in the centre here. Me and my husband have been quarrelling over it".

The husband interrupted cautiously "well . . . I don't really have an opinion on it darling".

The lady paused a moment, looked at me with a faint smile, and continued . . .

"Well I think these hanging bag-things look like the hanging bits of meat you find in a butchers. Would you agree?".

Before I had a chance to respond, she continued..

"You can still see them hanging from side to side can't you? Quite disturbing".

"They're not moving darling" the husband said sincerely.

"But look how they all move when I blow them".

She blew once and failed to disturb the inertia of the artwork, as if she were a small child trying to blow out all her birthday candles in one go. She continued to intervene in the secret dormant integrity of the object, stepping even closer and blowing even harder.

"See how they dance, see how light they are?" she replied happily.

The husband pulled himself upright from the wall he was leaning on and stepped closer to the work we were observing.

"You said they were hanging cattle a moment ago . . . and now they dance through the air?".

The wife gave him a sharp look.

"Well I have changed my mind, and quite rightly so. See how pure they are, set in white, presented so elegantly?"

I stepped in and began to lose myself a little-"I believe black to be the new white madam. It is all colours at once don't you know".

"Nonsense, it isn't even a colour!" the wife replied.

The husband, sensing that our conversation was becoming uneasy, decided to change the topic.

"I say, did you see any of the protests in town today? Do you know that they are planning to build a mosque here in Lincoln? There has been a ballot and permission has been granted. Well, this afternoon, hundreds of anti-Muslimism protesters, or anti-whatever protesters, marched through the streets and gathered at the place where the mosque will be built. And then a bunch of anti-racism protesters arrived. Can you imagine?! Police cars everywhere. Most of the town had to be shut off".

The wife replied with frustration-"Just what is the problem with building a mosque here? It is natural in this age to accom-modate for such things. And, of course, it will be beneficial to us in the end. Imagine how beautiful it will look?"

She glanced toward her husband and prodded him with a "darling?" He simply responded with a " . . . well . . . "

The wife continued; "And the imprudence of it all, only days after that poor muslim girl was found in the Brayford".

She took a few moments silence as if in repose . . . "decapitated, wrapped-up in a bin bag. Have you ever heard of such a thing?!"

The husband responded. "Well, they say that the reason so many people agreed to the building of the mosque, Muslim or non-Muslim, was because of the great sympathy people felt towards the young lady, Tracey Ohejav, the mosque being considered an act of condolence".

"Condolence!" The wife replied. "What on earth could be comforting about all of this?! An innocent woman was raped, stabbed, and then decapitated, wrapped in a black binliner and thrown into a river! Such a thing cannot be judged in relative terms. It was just a week ago when that poor soldier in London was..well, you know what I'm talking about".

I had stayed silent the whole time through this . . . conversation. Finally they noticed and looked at me as if I might wish to add something to their conversation.

"Well, perhaps now I see what you mean about the dynamic quality of the artwork. Yes, almost flamboyant. Perhaps, I mean, this is just a thought, it harks back to a type of Rococo fascination with form, the infinite folds indexed into the fabric-like sculptures connects to that distant world of Watteau's painted dresses. Definitely a sensibility more sublime and sensuous than that of the Modernists, the austere representation of that brute 'reality' they were trying so hard to capture, confined in the pseudo intellectual (and religious) white walls of the gallery space that demanded their appraisal. Perhaps it points to that dramatic white found in the interplay of light and dark conjured by the great chiaroscuro artist Caravaggio. Perhaps, if you really look hard enough, a glint of that white found in Vermeer's 'Milk Lady'. Yes, something milky, nutritious.. you can almost feel the northern renaissance beyond the alps, placing their stamp on the sensation here. . . . as if this present-day artist were saying that Europe, after all, was still to be looked upon as the future of the artistically cultivated man.. the man of *taste*. And on that note I must leave, as I have rudely barged in on your leisurely-some may say even quite passionate-conversation and company, so therefore I bid you good evening".

The husband and wife simply stared at me in a state of perplexity whilst unconsciously nodding. They continued watching me, as though I were in a silent film, wander out the door, pick the final glass of champagne up from the table, gulp it down in one and exit 'stage right' as it were.

Before successfully exiting down the hall and out of the building, I was again addressed by the lady at the front of house. This woman had become a small and persistent tumour to me. At base she was an ugly, fat, slow creature. No form to her, no signs of beauty nor agility; each layer of flesh lying on the next, squashed and pulled downwards by some unknown force like layers of sedimentary rock. I unfortunately and necessarily had to imagine her naked so as to clean her out (. . . of my mind?) and I understood, for a split second, why the Nazi's rid the Jews of all their clothes before torturing them. Because at the level of flesh we could simply disregard her, as a type of error, or some malignant deposit/residue between the real, true forms of the world that shine forth upon us. It could just be chipped-off, and then perhaps burnt, but the abscess has grown, through rearing, into a false sense of consciousness. And this is perhaps the worst part; when the base material has been dressed in silks and linens, given a hair brush, has teeth to clean . . . she might have even acquired shallow, deceptive desires that she gives time to before sleeping at night. Inside her brain, like a pin-ball machine-or a dog's brain-there is simply *custom*, a certain behaviour, a predetermined, conditioned personality. This is what life is presenting to me right now; the slow gradual lobotomy of itself, upon itself, forgetting with every cut that such actions, such intentions, comes from itself.

It was as if, with this lady, every movement, every action of thought, were being suppressed, pulled down into her thick dinosaur neck, given expression down there instead of anywhere celestial. She handed me a leaflet about the gallery and smiled at me as if *she* were smiling. But it was the world and her ignorance that formed this smile upon her lips. I avoided taking the pamphlet, saying nothing, pushing past her, wiping my now sweaty hands onto my trousers.

VIII

I WALKED UPHILL ON the cobbled path as if it were paved with burning coal, tiptoeing, skipping and jumping erratically like a dirty rat. I did not want the great gravity of torment to weigh me down. "Only a few steps to the cathedral, where all will be forgiven" I told myself. Police sirens were getting louder again, wrapping themselves around me. I was falling to the ground now, immersed in muddy gloom, but picking myself up, wading through the cobbles. Head spinning around, "is this the champagne? Why does my heart feel more religious the closer I am to getting caught? Am I in preparation for judgement? Why all this shit everywhere? Does God know I am the most important? Tracey is different now. She is stronger now. She wouldn't want this pity. Why are humans so full of pity? Let us think this thought *through* for once, 'philosophically' shall we say. Why do you feel pity for Tracey Ohejav? Well, you give death a bad name when you mourn over lost lives. Why make death an enemy? Pitying life's vulnerability to death? Pity?! That she was fortunate to be given birth to in the first place! From out of the indifferent infinity of atoms, molecules, eggs, sperm, under impossible conditions of life?! Tracey Ohejav *came through*! And she cried like all the rest of us, like every other human that has broken the skin of the earth, like a freshly popped blister taking to the air, sniffing out sanctimonious scents, vibrations, heat, beatitude".

Cathedral bells ring, crashing down, blow after blow, trickling like jewels slipping through the fingers of Midas. And they do not ask "in being born who did I take the place of?". Do you not see, that in this way we are all murderers!

And the only way to know *good* is through the wrong-doings of a man, picking-out and stumbling over all the naiveties of the world. How else would one know what is 'good' or not? The good is not already there in the first place, like water. It is found through consequences. The consequences that have *no* consequences, that is, those actions that only affect the human soul, through the grace of invisible guilt. These consequences do not linger about in the 'real' world of objects but fester in our minds as painful ghosts. That is the only way to learn, through *invisible guilt*. But in the end guilt is the same as pity, just turned inward.

No external event can ever truly judge you. Tracey was killed like an object. Fucked like an object. Today even the face is an object. When was the precise moment where we all put on our perennial masks? The face used to be everything to us; the flat, openness of the face, begging a response. A face that folded in on itself and gyrated like the expression found on childrens faces. The face that used to say four things.

1. "Do not kill me".

2. "Caress my face, cover my eye sockets gently with the palms of your hands or your lips".

3. "Nothing will help us from suffering" (look how soft a face is).

4. "Can you see God in my face?"

Tracey Ohejav didn't really have a face did she? It was all covered up. Just two black eyes, motionless, like an amphibian. Her eyes were too sharp; they looked out too much and seldom ever looked inside herself. Oh I feel incredibly sick now. Christ, you cannot love thy neighbour when they are all buffoons! But what am I saying?! I have been busy making and collecting things! Gathering materials for a new world! We can all be makers of our own world, yes?! And there is not an ounce of resentment in the act of creation. And Christ told me to do it . . . he picked me out. Perhaps I told myself to do it, the God of myself. And in this resurrection I have been born again? Or is it her that has been resurrected? I have been playing God with her haven't I? And will she love me now? Will he? We will soon find out.

At that precise moment I seemed to have started urinating inside my trousers. Urinating all over myself. I let the warm urine flow down my leg. I thought that I might be in Hell. I could see nothing. Blind. A black that did not depict depth or darkness but hung in front of me like an enormous clapperboard, or simply a block of matter. Living through such darkness I no longer seemed to live like a human. There was no action to be taken, no decision, no project one would even desire to fulfill. I breathed the exact same breaths (inhale/exhale), and these exact breaths returned to me eternally as if constantly recycling themselves. This new state would soon be acceptable to me. The atmosphere was sedating me. Soon I will have no memories or values. I will just exhale, look at my breath, and then inhale it again like a child playing with some primitive toy.

I had found in the past that each interaction with a human being brought about some worry, some thought, some responsibility. I am too sensitive to interact with people and harbour thoughts which attend them. Talking to people keeps me awake at night. I am not terribly fond of psychology you know. Worries come from out of the black like strange deep sea fishes. Two voices following one another.

At that precise moment I heard human voices, distant but clear. One of them said "that should be it", the other responding with "right you are". Immediately following this came four loud sounds;

kschh,
kschh,
kschh,
kickschh.

One by one each floodlight turned on and revealed a part of the cathedrals skin, making its way from the base of the cathedral to its spires. A journey of light covering eighty three metres. We are underwater, in a deep dark abyss, ebbing helplessly with one flashlight, the light picking up peculiar patches of details as we fall further. We are waiting for a light that is not ours, somewhere in the distance, or we are waiting for giant jaws to open, too tired to resist. I, the scuba diver, had found something in this dark abyss, with my torch. Like a giant octopus from the deep, sleeping dormant on the seabed, with old scaly skin like that of a whales. With treasure chests pushed into its belly, the most intricate stonework falling like dripping oil, guzzling itself to a rhythm akin to the breathing of a monster. The colour of old deserts mixed with the possibility of lost ruins farther out. I whispered to myself "I am not in hell . . . I am simply entering the jaws of it". Because of the absurdity of the earth and its lifeforms, heaven and hell become the same thing here.

I walked into the cathedral with my head down, deformed by powerlessness, like a schoolboy walking into the headmaster's office. I unbolted the latch and there before me lay a religious expanse.

IX

To the left, images depicting the succession of Genesis. Each painting fulfilling a certain role, confirming a certain destiny. They all affirm that such an archaic time happened here, upon the earth I now stumble upon. Is this realisation filled with the spirit of the world or is it merely historical reification? It is funny (. . . is it funny?) . . . I do not wish to talk to people about what they have done at work today. I do not even think of people highly enough to believe or respect their opinions (they are not your opinions). I wish even less to have to listen to the way they identify themselves with something or other. I would rather spend my time talking about this person Jesus Christ, and whether he was real or not. Whether he got jealous or not, what kind of dreams he had, what the funniest joke Paul told him was. Of course I know now that he existed. It takes an 'I' to be Jesus, and if one cannot comprehend and act on this then they are in the hands of God, they fall into the passivity of pure Being. And I saw this 'I' floating downstream, with arms held out, head bobbing in the water, as black as text.

I walked through the empty aisles and between the empty pews. I felt like the whole world was watching me. And outside the cathedral are humans oblivious to everything. Well there are some (very few) that know. There are some that know that deep down they are victims of a far-out impersonal cataclysm. They know that they are the burning of a distant star, fuelled by their own chaos and oblivion. And within this cataclysm, after time, being got steadier, more consistent. We even grew accustomed to it. And we called such being 'reality'. And this reality equated or corresponded to the things we learnt to see with our eyes, the information that we could process and possess. Soon all the chaos disappeared. Everything soon seemed to fit together through use and analogy; "that is for that", "that is this", "that means that". We groped around for the awareness of a Self through the analogy of various moments in experience and memory that all consist of a similar theme, angle, perspective. The inference of a 'cause' that will answer all questions, all grounds, all conditions. But this doesn't work does it? This cannot repress the beatitudes of unknowing, emotional yearning. All the developments of concept construction, all the mappings of descriptions onto objects, all the answers that 'put us in our place'. I am flying so high everyone, I am crying so much and I don't know why. And that is why my unique brain and the uniqueness of Christ can sense each other immediately. We are like two independent free spirits that only come together and acknowledge each other due to the stupidity of the situation. We are like two drunk men fighting in a bar who have to help each other up because the building is on fire, so for that brief moment we are civil (. . . we are still helping each other up!).

Hundreds of bibles inhabit this area of the cathedral. Some lean on each other, some pile-up on top of each other, some appear open on certain pages as if exhibiting their importance, some appear relaxed, open like a canyon yawn. One book is doing the splits on the floor.

I touch the stoney ground and it is cold. I forget why I am here yet I realise I have been here every day for the last three years. Every day, when I fall asleep, I dream that I walk into this cathedral at night, open the latch, walk between the empty aisles and pews, walk down a dark passage lit only by candles, and finally find a quiet place to die. How many times have I died before now? Will I really die this time, or, will I wake up?

I felt destined to walk down the candle-lit passage. I felt as though the whole world were watching me fall into a trap. "Not yet" I said to myself. I looked around for an exit, somewhere to hide. Like a child playing in a park, I was searching for an opening in the bushes, a hidden trail that would lead me out. Like a hidden door in a computer game, I scanned both left and right, even behind me, buffering the inevitable forward motion that beckoned me. Hiding between two angelic tombs, holding the sheer weight of history, I saw a Confession box. "I can talk my way out of this one" I said to myself. I walked in and took a deep breath.

X

I sit down and look up towards a little window, and I wait.

. . .

"Please kneel child of God".

I clumsily fall from my seat onto my knees.

"Have you come to ask God to help you know your sins"?

"God"?

. . .

"When was the last time you confessed and what sins do you accuse yourself of"?

"I confess daily. The language in my mind, the language I speak to others, is of a confessional nature. I accuse myself of taking someone's place when I was born. I accuse myself of stopping a normal healthy person from living, making money and having children. I accuse myself of being a renegade; of not respecting the values and laws of liberalism, capitalism, my society, my fellow citizens. But most of all I accuse myself of being unequalled by any man, I accuse myself of having taste, I accuse myself of being one of Christ's chosen ones".

Complete silence filled the confession box. The young man wondered if anyone, any priest, were really there. Either way, he felt as if he had got out what he had wanted to say. He had 'confessed'.

"Are you familiar with *The Epistle to the Romans*"? a voice whispered eventually, tunneling through the silence. "It is the sixth book in the new testament by Paul. In it Paul says;

'because that, when they knew God, they glorified him not as God, neither were thankful: but became vain in their imaginations, and their foolish heart was darkened. In professing oneself wise one becomes a fool'.

"I know that I am a fool. But to be a fool one must realise that they have been conned, been forsaken. This is more insight than the modern man has. He has been fooled time and time again but he doesn't see himself as a fool. How absolutely foolish that is! He is not even embarrassed by his state! Jesus was fooled. He died shouting 'Eloi, Eloi, Lama, Sabacthani!'. My God, my God, why hast thou forsaken me?".

The box was filled up with silence again, like water filling-up an ice cube tray.

The priest spoke . . .

"Quo Vadis"?

The young man replied "Quo Vadis?"

"Where are you going?" the priest said.

"I am not sure . . . but I feel as if I know or have once known. I am returning to somewhere . . . or am being told to go somewhere".

"*Quo Vadis* is what Jesus said to Peter when he began to flee Rome from likely crucifixion. You see, Jesus knew he was going to be crucified. He says "I am going to Rome to be crucified again", and this gives Peter courage to return to Rome with him, as martyrs. Jesus was not a fool, it was us who were the fools, it was us who didn't believe".

"Look here! Christ was forsaken, and I was forsaken! Aren't we all?! We are made up of abandonment. The burning stars have turned their back on us and have died out, we hover now in an empty abyss. The subconscious forsakes consciousness, and vice versa. The truth that should correspond to my soul has forsaken me and now I am left barren, picking up whatever fragments I can utilize to keep me alive. There is nothing in this world of me, of my image. All my expressions seem to stick to me, lay morbidly behind my glazed eyes, internally accumulating like mould".

More silence filled the confession box, but this time it felt mixed with disagreement and opinion.

"You remind me of a man, a young servant who stubbornly chose Jesus over God. He was a Roman, and at first he despised Jesus".

"We all hate Jesus first, it is the route to love, it is love's first guise".

"He reminds me of you" the priest continued. "He was antithetical to the Christian attitude. He thought that pity was a weakness in people, and that it was in fact condescending and rude. He had little time for social activities, much more time for personal development. He enjoyed power even though he was mainly victim to it. His name is derived from Greek and so he is that lovely mixture of Greco-Roman nobility which is particularly mysterious to Christians. I can see that you have this mystery inside you too. He was a servant, first to the Roman attitude, second to the Christian. Do you want to know the story?"

"Yes . . . I think I do".

"Malchus was the servant to the Jewish High Priest Caiaphas who participated in the arrest of Jesus. Malchus was ordered to apprehend Jesus and bring him to Rome to be judged by Pontius Pilate, with the help of a band of soldiers and, of course, Judas. At the moment when the soldiers were about to seize Jesus, St.Peter, out of anger, drew a sword from out of Malchus' scabbard and cut off the right ear of Malchus. Christ at once healed Malchus' wound out of benevolence and accepted his arrest where he was taken to Rome, whipped, given a crown of thorns, and later, crucified".

Malchus could hear the rustling of paper in the priest's compartment, through the tiny holes of the grid separating his tear drenched face from that of his Father.

"John. 18:10–11" . . .

> *Then Simon Peter having a sword drew it, and smote the high priest's servant, and cut off his right ear. The servant's name was Malchus.*
>
> *Then said Jesus unto Peter, Put up thy sword into the sheath: the cup which my Father hath given me, shall I not drink it?*

"It has been said that this was the last miracle of bodily cure that Christ made before his crucifixion. The last miracle was Malchus. Malchus converted to Christianity shortly after this, perhaps the first ever Roman to do so. This last miracle is you my boy".

Malchus replies sobbing "Gauguin takes my left ear and Peter takes my right. And both cheeks, slapped, on the left and then the right".

The priest interjects in a comforting voice.

"There is madness in everything Malchus. There is madness in all the bloodlines. There is madness in Caligula's insanity on the beach. There is a madness in Nero, capturing Christians dipped in oil, setting them on fire in his garden at night as a source of light. There is madness in our favourite apostles; Paul was indeed preoccupied with a form of madness. There would have been a madness in the first Christians seen by the Romans; they worship *a man* as God, they practice monotheism, they are accused of incest and cannibalism. Madness is the only true way to be . . . you just have to choose the side that you want to win".

Malchus removes the hands that cradle his creased and wet face.

"Forgive me father for I have sinned".

Silence began to fill up the room again. Silence breathed again. A different silence, a resolute silence. All the different silences between the most tragic acts in the history of the world. The silence before Robespierre was guillotined, with his face upwards towards the blade. The silence between the flames of Giordano Bruno before he was burnt at the stake. Every silence ever imparted, every silence withdrawing itself, every silence offering up action. All romantic silences, all silences in nature, all religious silences, awkward silences, guilty silences, imposed silences, silences filling up new houses on the market, old attics, the silence of a letter in an unopened envelope . . .

XI

"It was Friday, April the third. I was walking down the canal, towards the town. It was around midnight. In the distance I could see three figures walking erratically, like dirty rats. The middle, smaller figure, was screaming. It was a woman, and I was under the impression that she was either drunk or flirting. But the screams grew more disturbing, more imminent. The movement of her body was vicious, jerking side to side between the two larger figures who now appeared to be men. She was being pulled to and fro like a dog. The woman shrieked and squealed in a language of screams that I had not heard before. They were religious screams, becoming lower in tone, more sombre. I did not want to be noticed. I hid inside an abandoned garage that I was passing by. The door was already half open, half agape, as if it were observing an act of horrendous evil. I crawled under the garage door and pulled the rest of it down behind me.

I stood with my back against the cold metal door, my heart beating ferociously. I stared into a black abyss similar to this confessional box we converse in. I tried to stop breathing and listened deeply to whatever stimuli lay outside of my box. The woman's religious screams were now mixed with tears. Tears muffling her words, dribbling down her nose. I could almost hear the sound of them hit the pavement one by one. I could hear the men now. The sound of the left-inside of their denim jeans rubbing against the right. The sound of boots or trainers clumsily putting weight onto the ground. The woman was not wearing high heels but flat soled shoes that stroked the ground as they were dragged along carelessly by the two men. I could hear something rattle, some embellishment worn on a dress, a clip within her hair, a bracelet jangling-but made of wood or plastic-not metal. The men's clothes made no other sounds, they were stupid drunk murderers. They wake up and place a t-shirt over their protruding gut, baggy blue jeans to cover their pale, ugly, childish and humiliating legs.

I want so badly to hear the sounds of other people, a group of students, a man on his bicycle cycling home . . . but nothing. Not even nature had the courage to speak up, to apprehend. Nature could not even comprehend.

The woman's bracelet fell off and I could hear the sound of tiny jewels rolling away, scattering, becoming part of that sparkle one can sometimes see on a pavement in summer.

Every accessory of integrity drooped and fell off Tracey Ohejav. It was then that her body was pushed into the garage door, the door of the garage I was hiding within. The sound crashed off every wall and momentarily deafened me. I could not hear. My ears were cut off from the rest of the world. Without sound I accepted a new level of touch. Tracey's body had made an indentation on the thin steel garage door separating myself from the crime. Perhaps my own body, with its back against the internal side of the door, had buffered her impact. For that one moment we were leaning on one another; me, a silly sensitive fool, and her, an innocent woman who was about to be raped and decapitated. If I had known her name at that moment I would have whispered "I love you Tracey Ohejav".

After the initial crash of her fragile body into the garage door, others began. I only knew this because I could feel the thin steel door dig into my back, my ears still ringing. Over and over again the door protruded into my back. Every thrust into Tracey the men took, I could feel her back touch mine. Touching mine in a delicate way, with grace, saying "It is ok, all will be over soon, we will be together and keep each other safe through this random act of senseless violence".

"Perhaps we could pretend that *we* were making love, Tracey? And I would rest you delicately onto something soft, lightly push the hair back from across your face to behind your ears. I would look at you in the eyes, from above, and we would make love. No fucking and no raping".

As my ears began to pick up sound again I could hear the same lines whirring in my head, repeating as if on a broken loop. I could still retrace the sound to Tracey .. but soon there would be no trace of Tracey. The words were *Eloi Eloi Lama Sabacthani.*

I sat down in the cold garage and quietly wept. Tracey's broken body was picked up by the two men and dragged away. Again I could hear the soft soles of her shoes caress everything in its path; broken glass, half-smoked cigarettes, strange insects .. perhaps a ladybird.

I opened the garage door at around 4 am. The morning sun broke into the concrete box almost immediately. I arose from what felt like a cave, rising from the dead. Tracey's body and head floated past me, trapped in flora. Also, violets, nettles, daisies, and what seemed to be a poppy followed her downstream. I had to save her somehow".

XII

SILENCE FILLED THE CONFESSIONAL box again. The silence weighed heavier on the priest, as if he were struggling for words to say.

"God bless you Malchus . . . but you must impart this information to the police. It could help them with the case".

"The police! I am sat here confessing to the only man worthy of offering me penance, and he offers me up to the police! I do not obey the police, they are guiltier than me. In fact they wouldn't know the difference between freedom and servitude! Priest . . . why couldn't you have been my *friend*?"

The priest responded-"I am your friend Malchus".

More silence followed as if it were changing its mind about something.

"Do you know that they have caught the two men who killed her?"

"Killed her and raped her. . . . Yes I have read about it".

"How do you know that it was the same girl?"

"It happened at the same time and place. How many people get raped and decapitated in Lincoln?!"

"Do you know if the men who did this match the photographs in the papers?"

"I never saw the men. I never saw Tracey . . . until afterwards . . . but seamen was found in Tracey Ohejav that matches one of the men convicted. Seamen would have been found in her mouth too if they had retrieved it".

. . .

"You couldn't have saved her boy. I'm sorry you had to witness that".

"You are wrong. I did save her".

Another silence ensued. This silence said "it is time to go home".

Malchus looked tired now.

"Do you not see? I am not here to repent for anything that happened to Tracey. I am not guilty for anything that happened to her. I told you this out of joy. They were tears of joy and not sadness . . . not weakness. I wanted to talk about my guilt and my suffering, from being in this world, at this time, under these values and laws, but instead I am telling you how great I am and how I saved Tracey. This is a joke. What does a Christian have to do to get a good confession around here? I am done! I don't need to feel guilty. This epoch *has not found it yet*. This world has not discovered guilt for me to even *be* guilty. Perhaps I should *enjoy myself*. That is what you people do best don't you? Or you pretend to enjoy yourself under strict laws and timeframes. The leisure industry, side by side with the work industry. One door closes as the other one opens. No one ever realized they were ruled by the same determinacy-the law of leisure, the law of entertainment. Perhaps I should have killed Tracey Ohejav. Perhaps those criminals are the only ones really living; subverting laws, subverting experience, *testing* themselves and their conscience. All sensation is a violence of some sort, all overcoming is a form of domination.

. . .

Do not worry though priest. I will always love the cross. I will love all the aesthetics of Christianity. It is one of my *styles*. It is a *taste* of some sort. And I will leave you these keys as a token of my appreciation to you . . . 'priest'. Garage 3C, opposite the dustbins, Dixon Street. I hope Lincoln will find art and culture again in the near future. I hope Britain does in-fact! But for me-I'm going to a place where the climate is more suited to me, a clearer air, a place where I can drink water straight from a spring or fountain, a place where the colours are real and not printed onto things.

XII

OUTSIDE OF OUR THOUGHTS, or when all our thoughts have disappeared, is there still a world? I used to find comfort in the fact that it would still rain, leaves would still fall, regardless of whatever I was thinking, whatever private world I was immersed in, but now I'm not so sure.

When I think of Nature, let us say when I think of a boulder, what first comes to mind is a drawing of a boulder, a cartoon in-fact, perhaps from the Flintstones . . . or Charlie Brown. I remember watching these cartoons at home whilst my father was at church. This is my 'default' go-to 'boulder' in my memory bank. My memory is made up of drawings, cartoons, paintings and photographs. This is one of the things that Malchus taught me; that the world rarely has its own colours, that one can't get beyond the image of nature *to* nature.

Words too also jostle in my head and fight for their right of place, to fall out of my mouth, to communicate to the world what 'I' am thinking and feeling. But words are like boulders in this respect. I do not know if they were ever right, if they ever truly connected to the experiences I have had, have had to endure. What can a word know about a sudden rush of the heart, what can a word know about rape and decapitation, what can a word know about silence? I look up towards the sky. It is early morning. I reach garage 3C and unlock the door.

XIII

Unbearable white sunlight broke into garage 3C. Did the light rays intrude or were they simply desperate to return back to the garage, as if hungry dogs stampeding the entrance of their home at the smell of food? There was no doubt that Jesus had been here. Something secret, profound and dangerous was ready to burst out of this garage, as if contained, intolerably, for so long. The burst would be more like a blossom than an explosion. It would be a silent alarm. In-fact it is only silence, our silence, that would comprehend it.

A woman stood upright in the far left hand corner of the space. She was perfectly at peace with herself, perfectly composed, singing the most exquisite, harmonious choral music I had ever heard. Her voice was soft and sometimes it would crackle, but within the notes there disclosed enormous complexity and depth. A dress covered this woman, black, beautiful and understated. Her face, an amalgamation of all those unobtainable ideals of beauty and purity that every portrait artist has attempted to catch, yet at the same time, peasant-like, simple, unique. Her lips were rose-coloured, and even scented. Around her wrist lay a bracelet made up of intertwined daisies. In the far right hand corner a simple duvet and pillow sprawled itself out.

The four walls of this garage contain a room so small, yet it feels infinitely deep and spacious to me now. It reflects my own subjectivity, at once atomistic and absolute. I am not sure how I got here. My title suggests I am a man to be respected, revered, but being in this room I feel as though I were a boy again, being led through the dark and mysterious rooms of a local museum I had frequented as a child. I was always led, hand in hand, by my father. But somewhere down the line I broke off from his grip. I walked down the dark passages of the museum hesitantly on my own. The alien artefacts, illuminated from within the glass cabinets that stored them, made me lose all sense of myself. Only curiosity survived. The museum itself made me just another anomalous object among objects. I was part of the uncanny. I felt as though the world were a swamp of strange detritus and that life should be lived through stages of exploring (or enduring) the unknown.

The sun is soaking into everything now. It seems that I am but a man in a garage, and these two words 'man' and 'garage' can be infinitely interchangeable with any other number of words without anything drastically changing. I found that a smile had rested upon my face. I always seem to find some solace, some joy in the sheer complicity of the human condition. This is why I am a reverend, because I obviously have some form of psychological faith in the notion that 'everything is secretly ok'. I must walk back to the Cathedral. I must start again, like I do everyday. To understand. I waved goodbye to the woman and closed the door, before handing-in the key to the local police station.

XIV

To: ALL MEDIA ORGANIZATIONS and other persons submitting Requests for Records pursuant to the Retention and Disclosure of all Police documents that are in keeping with the Freedom of Information Act (2000).

Enclosed herewith are the following documents: (i) the Incident Report pertaining to the incident occurring on April 16, 2016; (ii) the dispatch logs showing the time of events commencing with Reverend Friedrich's statement; and (iii) still photos taken by myself (see fig 1,2 and 3).

Lastly, certain information had been redacted from the Incident Report and has been deemed closed under Section A.D.30. 16.04.

My Report;

Arrived at Garage 3C, Dixon Street, Lincoln, LN5 8JA at 9 A.M. Area 112.4 N.E, N.S (the entirety of the garage lots) have been identified, isolated and secured. Access has been restricted. Testimonial evidence has been given by Reverend Friedrich (see Document 2 for statement and Contact Details). Physical evidence inside garage 3C are as follows;

> A manikin stand with torso and arms is stood upright in the far left hand corner of the garage. Over the manikin torso is a black bin-bag with holes cut out either side for each of the arms to fit through. Above the manikin torso is the head of Tracey Ohejav (see Document 3 for Photographs Presented and Chief Medical Examiner Confirmation). The head has been painted with watercolour paints

resembling makeup (possibly to cover up the physical de-composition of the face or for aesthetic reasons). Rose pet-als have been placed in her mouth. There is a long tear in the left ear (made with considerable force it would seem). Below the manikin, on the floor to the right, is a wind-up Gramophone record player. A record has been placed on it and the stylus is still sitting on the record. A piece of carefully cut card has been placed below the base of the manikin stand. It reads;

Tracey Ohejav-Still Life, Portrait and Sculpture-Mixed Media-AD 30/2016.

Please note; her ear has been cut away because she is an Artist, she is Roman, She is a Christian, and because she does NOT want to hear sirens anymore.

With Love,
Malchus

XV

I AM MALCHUS. I am ancient ivory. I am white pillars. I am all dreams and also what dreams do not know. I am Malchus. I am a clearing of the throat, a nervous tick, a stumble. I am Malchus. I make all disgusting and base things perfectly so. I am Malchus. I am the disease of time, it's rotting, from purity to decadence. I am Malchus. I am waiting for nothing but you, to turn into nothing. I am Malchus. I am every hot summer's day where all children haunt the streets and break soft flowers, but I am also those who stay inside, in the shade, doing nothing but quietly remembering and crying. I am Malchus, I am a detail, an error, that affects and transforms the initial cause. I am Malchus. I am that moment when you realise, on your deathbed, that you have lived the wrong life. I am Malchus. I am the vast vistas of impersonal distance, not in the cosmos but between two sets of eyes that happen to glance upon each other. I am Malchus. I am the lobster waiting to be eaten in the tank in the restuarant that you dine in, the food that misses your mouth, that you wipe with a napkin and fold in order to hide. I am Malchus, I am not what you are. I am Malchus. I am not a value, I am not tolerable, I am the sweat of every anxious man. I am Malchus. I am a noisy silence that lingers, like the ticking of clocks, like rubble falling off a cliff, like the panting of an overweight child. I am Malchus. I am where all hope is revealed as a futile projection. I am Machus. I am reflections of reflections of reflections. I am Malchus. I do not speak, I do not open the mouth, instead I cut constantly, my very being is so sharp that it loses itself on its own edge and returns as a fine line. I am Malchus. I am every angry child, walking through a cemetery in the morning, towards their school. I am Malchus. I am a father who does not know his own father or even the concept of one. I am Malchus, I thought I was not Malchus but I am Malchus. I am Malchus. I am the moment of ejaculation but also the moment where you turn your head away. I am Malchus. I am every mentally handicapped child laughing in your head. I am also the cause of their laughter. I am Malchus. I am what you are yet turned into art. I am Malchus. I am something that fights constantly over other fighting things. I am Malchus. I am trying to understand myself through the suffering context of everyone else. I am Machus. I am the moment just before you fall asleep. I am your duvet and your pillow. I am Malchus. I am at the forefront of your mind, I am the word that you read, yet I am the word that means nothing. I am Malchus.

Lightning Source UK Ltd
Milton Keynes UK
UKOW01f2311060917
308723UK00004B/367/P